STOP SNORING, BERNARD!

ZACHARIAH OHORA

HENRY HOLT AND COMPANY
NEW YORK

With special thanks
to Robin Tordini

Henry Holt and Company, LLC
Publishers since 1866
175 Fifth Avenue
New York, New York 10010
www.HenryHoltKids.com

Distributed in Canada by H. B. Fenn and Company Ltd.

Library of Congress Cataloging-in-Publication Data
OHora, Zachariah.
Stop snoring, Bernard! / Zachariah OHora. — 1st ed.
p.   cm.
Summary: Because his loud snores disturb all the other animals
at the zoo, Bernard the otter tries to find a solution.
ISBN 978-0-8050-9002-4
[1. Otters—Fiction. 2. Snoring—Fiction. 3. Zoo animals—Fiction.
4. Zoos—Fiction.] I. Title.
PZ7.O41405St 2010   [E]—dc22   2009005265

First Edition—2011 / Designed by Véronique Lefèvre Sweet
Printed in January 2011 in China by C&C Joint Printing Co.,
Shenzhen, Guangdong Province, on acid-free paper. ∞
The artwork was painted in acrylic on 100-percent cotton rag 120-pound
Stonehenge paper.

10 9 8 7 6 5 4 3 2 1

To Lydia, my love

Bernard loved living at the zoo.
He loved mealtime, playtime,
and best of all . . .

. . . naptime!

But there was one little problem.
Bernard snored . . . LOUDLY!

One afternoon at naptime,
Grumpy Giles had had enough.
"Snore somewhere else,
Bernard!" he said.

Bernard tried sleeping in a lake, but that didn't work.

He tried sleeping in a fountain,
but that didn't work either.

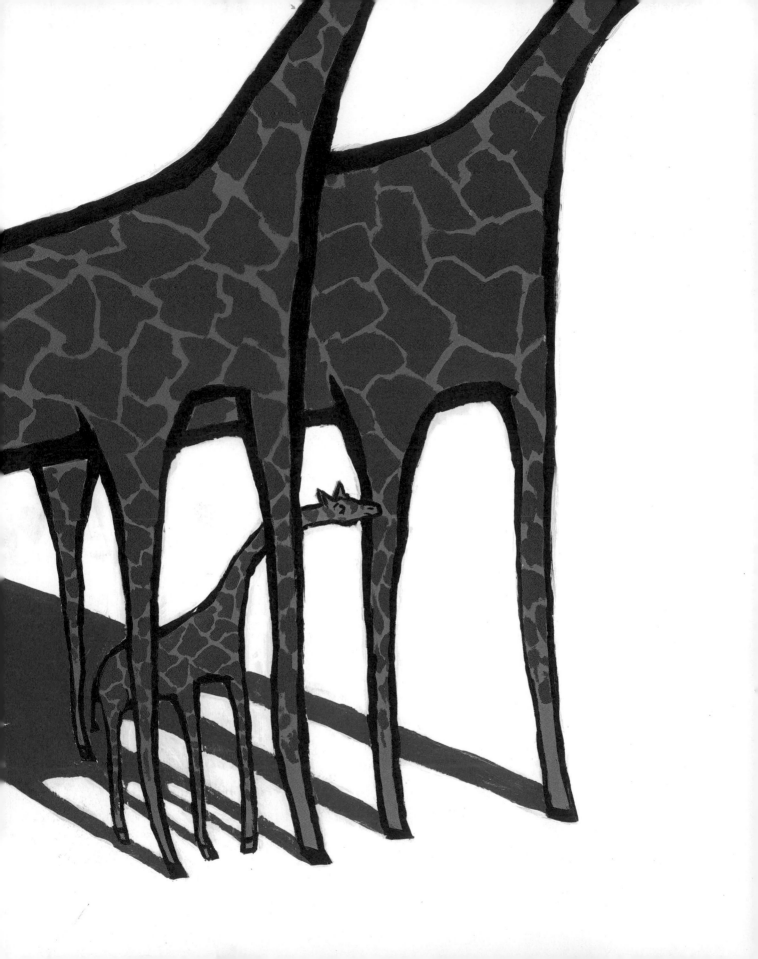

He even tried sleeping in a puddle!
But that *really* didn't work.

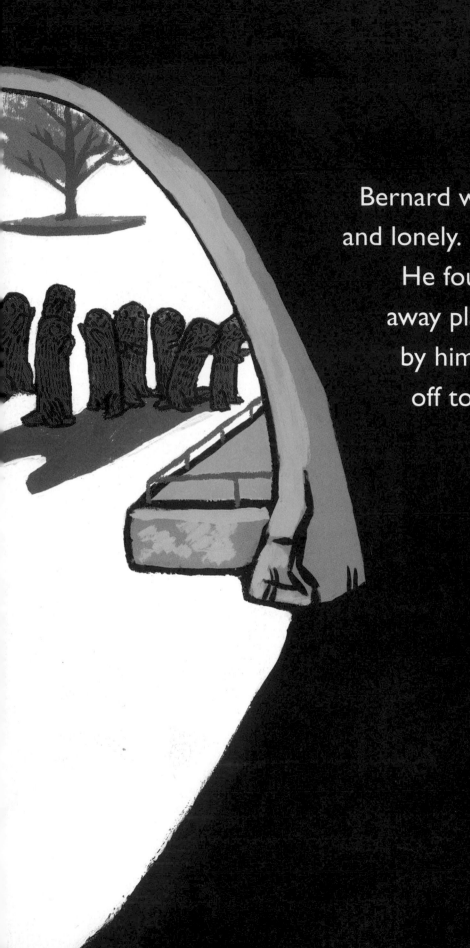

Bernard was sad
and lonely.
He found a tucked-
away place, curled up
by himself, and drifted
off to sleep.

The other otters missed Bernard.
They searched for him all through
the night.

The next morning Bernard woke up and
saw hundreds of bats on the ceiling.

"Excuse me!" he said. "How did you
sleep with all my snoring?"

"We didn't," replied a bat. "We were out
all night and now we are trying to sleep. So
please don't snore here."

Bernard felt terrible. There wasn't anyplace
he could sleep without bothering somebody.
He trudged toward the zoo gate.
But then he heard something.

It was the other otters!

"We couldn't sleep without you," said Grumpy Giles. "And I'm sorry I yelled. Please come back."

And from that day on, everyone napped happily. Well, almost everyone.